✔ KU-286-742

THIS BOOK

BELONGS TO:

......................................................

......................................................

# THE TALE OF
## *Squirrel Nutkin*

# THE TALE OF
# SQUIRREL NUTKIN

BY

BEATRIX POTTER

FREDERICK WARNE

FREDERICK WARNE

Published by the Penguin Group
Penguin Books Ltd, 80 Strand, London WC2R ORL, England
Penguin Putnam Inc., 375 Hudson Street, New York, New York 10014, USA
Penguin Books Australia Ltd, 250 Camberwell Road, Camberwell, Victoria 3124, Australia
Penguin Books Canada Ltd, 10 Alcorn Avenue, Toronto, Ontario, Canada M4V 3B2
Penguin Books India (P) Ltd, 11 Community Centre,
Panchsheel Park, New Delhi 110 017, India
Penguin Books (NZ) Ltd, Cnr Rosedale and Airborne Roads,
Albany, Auckland, New Zealand
Penguin Books (South Africa) (Pty) Ltd, PO Box 9, Parklands 2121, South Africa

Penguin Books Ltd, Registered Offices: 80 Strand, London WC2R ORL, England

Web site at: www.peterrabbit.com

First published by Frederick Warne 1903
This edition with reset text and new reproductions of Beatrix Potter's
illustrations first published 2002

New reproductions copyright ©Frederick Warne & Co., 2002
Original copyright in text and illustrations ©Frederick Warne & Co., 1903
Frederick Warne & Co. is the owner of all rights, copyrights and trademarks
in the Beatrix Potter character names and illustrations.

All rights reserved. Without limiting the rights under copyright reserved
above, no part of this publication may be reproduced, stored in or introduced
into a retrieval system, or transmitted in any form or by any means
(electronic, mechanical, photocopying, recording or otherwise), without the
prior written permission of the above publisher of this book.

Colour reproduction by
EAE Creative Colour Ltd, Norwich
Printed and bound in Italy

1102

A STORY FOR NORAH

THIS IS A TALE about a tail — a tail that belonged to a little red squirrel, and his name was Nutkin.

He had a brother called Twinkleberry, and a great many cousins; they lived in a wood at the edge of a lake.

In the middle of the lake there is an island covered with trees and nut bushes; and amongst those trees stands a hollow oak-tree, which is the house of an owl who is called Old Brown.

ONE autumn when the nuts were ripe, and the leaves on the hazel bushes were golden and green — Nutkin and Twinkleberry and all the other little squirrels came out of the wood, and down to the edge of the lake.

THEY made little rafts out of twigs, and they paddled away over the water to Owl Island to gather nuts.

Each squirrel had a little sack and a large oar, and spread out his tail for a sail.

THEY also took with them an offering of three fat mice as a present for Old Brown, and put them down upon his doorstep.

Then Twinkleberry and the other little squirrels each made a low bow, and said politely —

"Old Mr. Brown, will you favour us with permission to gather nuts upon your island?"

BUT Nutkin was excessively impertinent in his manners. He bobbed up and down like a little red *cherry*, singing —

"Riddle me, riddle me, rot-tot-tote!
 A little wee man, in a red red coat!
 A staff in his hand, and a stone in his throat;
 If you'll tell me this riddle, I'll give you a groat."

Now this riddle is as old as the hills; Mr. Brown paid no attention whatever to Nutkin.

He shut his eyes obstinately and went to sleep.

THE squirrels filled their little sacks with nuts, and sailed away home in the evening.

BUT next morning they all came back again to Owl Island; and Twinkleberry and the others brought a fine fat mole, and laid it on the stone in front of Old Brown's doorway, and said—

"Mr. Brown, will you favour us with your gracious permission to gather some more nuts?"

BUT Nutkin, who had no respect, began to dance up and down, tickling old Mr. Brown with a *nettle* and singing —

"Old Mr. B! Riddle-me-ree!
Hitty Pitty within the wall,
Hitty Pitty without the wall;
If you touch Hitty Pitty,
Hitty Pitty will bite you!"

Mr. Brown woke up suddenly and carried the mole into his house.

HE shut the door in Nutkin's face. Presently a little thread of blue *smoke* from a wood fire came up from the top of the tree, and Nutkin peeped through the key-hole and sang —

"A house full, a hole full!
And you cannot gather a bowl-full!"

THE squirrels searched for nuts all over the island and filled their little sacks.

But Nutkin gathered oak-apples — yellow and scarlet — and sat upon a beech-stump playing marbles, and watching the door of old Mr. Brown.

On the third day the squirrels got up very early and went fishing; they caught seven fat minnows as a present for Old Brown.

They paddled over the lake and landed under a crooked chestnut tree on Owl Island.

TWINKLEBERRY and six other little squirrels each carried a fat minnow; but Nutkin, who had no nice manners, brought no present at all. He ran in front, singing —

"The man in the wilderness said to me,
 'How many strawberries grow in the sea?'
 I answered him as I thought good—
 'As many red herrings as grow in the wood.'"

But old Mr. Brown took no interest in riddles — not even when the answer was provided for him.

ON the fourth day the squirrels brought a present of six fat beetles, which were as good as plums in *plum-pudding* for Old Brown. Each beetle was wrapped up carefully in a dock-leaf, fastened with a pine-needle pin.

But Nutkin sang as rudely as ever —

"Old Mr. B! Riddle-me-ree!
Flour of England, fruit of Spain,
Met together in a shower of rain;
Put in a bag tied round with a string,
If you'll tell me this riddle, I'll give you a ring!"

Which was ridiculous of Nutkin, because he had not got any ring to give to Old Brown.

THE other squirrels hunted up
and down the nut bushes; but
Nutkin gathered robin's pin-
cushions off a briar bush, and
stuck them full of pine-needle
pins.

ON the fifth day the squirrels brought a present of wild honey; it was so sweet and sticky that they licked their fingers as they put it down upon the stone. They had stolen it out of a bumble *bees'* nest on the tippitty top of the hill.

But Nutkin skipped up and down, singing—

"Hum-a-bum! buzz! buzz! Hum-a-bum buzz!
As I went over Tipple-tine
I met a flock of bonny swine;
Some yellow-nacked, some yellow backed!
They were the very bonniest swine
That e'er went over Tipple-tine."

OLD Mr. Brown turned up his eyes in disgust at the impertinence of Nutkin.

But he ate up the honey!

THE squirrels filled their little sacks with nuts.

But Nutkin sat upon a big flat rock, and played ninepins with a crab apple and green fir-cones.

ON the sixth day, which was Saturday, the squirrels came again for the last time; they brought a new-laid *egg* in a little rush basket as a last parting present for Old Brown.

But Nutkin ran in front laughing, and shouting—

"Humpty Dumpty lies in the beck,
 With a white counterpane round his neck,
 Forty doctors and forty wrights,
 Cannot put Humpty Dumpty to rights!"

Now old Mr. Brown took an interest in eggs; he opened one eye and shut it again. But still he did not speak.

NUTKIN became more and more impertinent —

"Old Mr. B! Old Mr. B!
Hickamore, Hackamore,
    on the King's kitchen door;
All the King's horses,
    and all the King's men,
Couldn't drive Hickamore, Hackamore,
Off the King's kitchen door!"

Nutkin danced up and down like a *sunbeam*; but still Old Brown said nothing at all.

NUTKIN began again —

"Arthur O'Bower has broken his band,
He comes roaring up the land!
The King of Scots with all his power,
Cannot turn Arthur of the Bower!"

Nutkin made a whirring noise
to sound like the *wind*, and he
took a running jump right onto
the head of Old Brown! . . .

Then all at once there was a
flutterment and a scufflement
and a loud "Squeak!"

The other squirrels scuttered
away into the bushes.

49

WHEN they came back very
cautiously, peeping round the
tree — there was Old Brown
sitting on his door-step, quite
still, with his eyes closed, as if
nothing had happened.

*

*But Nutkin was in his waist-
coat pocket!*

THIS looks like the end of the story; but it isn't.

OLD BROWN carried Nutkin into his house, and held him up by the tail, intending to skin him; but Nutkin pulled so very hard that his tail broke in two, and he dashed up the staircase, and escaped out of the attic window.

AND to this day, if you meet Nutkin up a tree and ask him a riddle, he will throw sticks at you, and stamp his feet and scold, and shout —

"Cuck-cuck-cuck-cur-r-r-cuck-k-k!"

THE END